PORTRAITS
of LITTLE WOMEN

A Gift
for Amy

Don't miss any of the
Portraits of Little Women

PORTRAITS
of LITTLE WOMEN

A Gift
for Amy

Susan Beth Pfeffer

DELACORTE PRESS

Published by
Delacorte Press
a division of Random House, Inc.
1540 Broadway
New York, New York 10036

Library of Congress Cataloging-in-Publication Data

Cataloging-in-publication data is
available from the Library of Congress.

ISBN: 0-385-32671-8

The text of this book is set in 13-point Cochin.

Book design by Patrice Sheridan
Cover art © 1999 by Lori Earley
Text art © 1999 by Marcy Ramsey
Activities art © 1999 by Laura Maestro

Manufactured in the United States of America

July 1999

10 9 8 7 6 5 4 3 2 1

BVG

TO SAM AND LINDA PROCTOR

CONTENTS

CHAPTER 1

"Don't spend all your time staring into that hand mirror," Jo March said to her youngest sister, Amy. "Vanity's one of the seven deadly sins, you know."

Amy sighed. Jo was so annoying, always teasing her, always telling her what she did wrong. Besides, she wasn't being vain. The exact opposite, really. Amy was staring into the mirror wishing she were beautiful.

Jo rolled her eyes. "How the poor child suffers," she said.

"Now, Jo, stop your teasing," Meg said, following Jo into Amy's bedroom. "We all know vanity is a sin, but sometimes a girl simply has to look in a mirror."

"I never do," Jo said. "Neither does Beth, I'm sure."

Amy snorted. "You're such a liar, Jo March," she said. "And lying is a deadly sin too. You look in the mirror every day, admiring that long mane of hair you have." She was pleased to see Jo blush. It was tiresome being the youngest in the family and always in the wrong. When she scored a point against any of her sisters, Jo in particular, Amy enjoyed it.

Even Meg and Beth laughed, which only made Amy feel better. "She has you there, Jo," Meg said. "You do love to look at your hair."

"Jo has beautiful hair," Beth said from her bed, where she was sitting with her mending. "Amy does also. And Meg is so pretty. I'm surprised you don't all spend each day staring into the mirror."

"We would if we had enough mirrors," Meg said, and this time Amy laughed as well.

"I'm sure the girls at school admire themselves all the time," Amy said.

"That's why they don't know their lessons," Jo replied. "And why they don't think of others. And why—"

"And why they look so pretty," said Meg. "Vanity may be a sin, but envy is also, and I'm afraid I suffer from that."

"I suffer from the sin of contrariness," said Jo. "If that isn't a deadly sin, it surely should be."

"And I'm cowardly," Beth said. "Perhaps that's not deadly to others, but it is deadly to me."

Amy felt her sisters' eyes turn to her. She knew she was supposed to say what her own particular sin was, but she wasn't in the mood. "I strive for perfection," she said instead, but she didn't mind when her sisters laughed.

"You're smart and you're pretty," Jo said. "You're talented, too, much as I hate to admit it. But you have quite a way to go before you hit perfection."

"We all do," Meg said. "I don't know about you, Jo, but I have my doubts I'll ever achieve it."

"I'd settle for greatness," answered Jo. "I'm sure Shakespeare had his share of sins, but oh, what glorious poetry he wrote."

"Did you mean what you said?" Amy asked. "That I'm pretty and smart and talented?"

Jo smiled. "Perhaps. But you are the one who accused me of being a liar."

"Jo," Meg said sharply. "She meant it, Amy. You *are* smart and pretty and talented."

"And good," said Beth. "People like you, Amy. You have so many friends."

"But you'll lose them if you spend all your time in front of a mirror," said Jo.

"Besides," Meg said, "we all like to have our time at the mirror. It's not fair for any one of us to hold on to it."

What wasn't fair was that four girls had to share one mirror, Amy thought. Hand-me-downs weren't fair. Being poor wasn't fair.

"I wish Father were still at home," Beth said. "I know it's wrong of me to wish that when he's doing such good work with our soldiers, but I miss him so."

"We all do," said Jo. "What makes you mention him now, Bethy?"

"The mirror," Beth replied. "I remember one afternoon when Father found me staring into it. I don't know why I was so fascinated by my image that day, but I couldn't tear my eyes away from it. When Father saw me, I was sure he'd scold me, the way you were scolding Amy, Jo. But he just kissed my forehead and said there was no mirror powerful enough to show the goodness of my soul. I know he'd say just the same thing to Amy."

"Father always knows just what to say," Meg declared. "I miss him all the time also."

"Marmee misses him the most," Jo said. "We should all try harder to get along and do more to make things easier for her."

"You're right," Meg said. "I'll try harder to make do. Though I do wish I had pretty dresses and new shoes."

"I wish I didn't have to spend so much time with Aunt March," Jo said. She had just begun

5

to work as Aunt March's companion, and she came home each evening complaining about what the elderly woman demanded of her.

"I wish we were rich," Amy said. "And that I was beautiful and had men pursuing me. Rich men. And that I lived in a mansion and had lots of servants. And jewelry. Diamonds and emeralds. And horses. And a coach, like Aunt March's. And trips abroad and seasons in New York. And I'd like to be famous as well, known far and wide as a great artist, with my work in museums. And I'd like to have so many dresses of silk and lace that I'd need an entire room to hold them."

"The better to go with your diamonds and emeralds," said Jo.

This time it was Amy's turn to blush. "I know I sound foolish," she said.

"Foolish and greedy," said Jo. "And you're only ten years old."

"You have foolish and greedy dreams of your own," said Amy. "You want to be compared with Shakespeare."

"I do have a long way to go," Jo said, cheerfully enough. "But my last play, *Count Alessandro's Fatal Secret*, was my best ever. And Amy, you were quite good in it. I wish Father could have seen it. He always thought you were a gifted actress."

Suddenly Amy wished for nothing more than the safe return of her father. He never teased her. Even when he scolded her, she knew it was because he loved her. "Do you think he'll come home safely?" she asked.

"I'm sure of it," said Jo.

"I am also," Meg said. "It would be too horrible if anything happened to him."

The sisters sat quietly for a moment. Then Beth laughed. "That mirror really is powerful," she said. "Think of all it's made us admit to today."

"You know, you're right," said Jo. "I should use the mirror as a plot in my next play. It could have supernatural powers. It could reveal the truth about people's souls."

"There she goes," said Meg. "You might not be the writer Shakespeare was, Jo, but you certainly have as much of an imagination."

7

"That's because my sisters are so inspiring," Jo said. "Now I think I'll run up to the attic and scribble down the idea while I have the chance. And tomorrow, when Aunt March dozes off, I'll have time to work on it in my head, at least."

"I'll go downstairs and help Marmee," Meg said. "Which was where I was planning to go before I got distracted by all this mirror talk."

Amy was glad when her sisters left. It was bad enough sharing her bedroom with Beth, but when Meg and Jo were there also, Amy was even more painfully aware of how small her room really was.

"Did you honestly look at yourself in the mirror?" she asked Beth.

Beth nodded. "Sometimes I feel as if people don't see me," she said. "I think I wanted the mirror to tell me why."

"People see you," Amy said. "And they love you because you're so good. It's just that you're shy."

"I wish I weren't," Beth said. "I'd like to be more like you, Amy. Outgoing, with friends."

8

Amy put down the mirror and looked at her sister. She knew she should say she wanted to be more like Beth, sweet and kind. But she didn't. She wanted to be beautiful and talented and rich. And somehow she doubted that being sweet and kind was the way she'd achieve all she wanted.

CHAPTER 2

"What a pretty brooch, Diana," Amy said the next day before school began.

"Thank you," Diana Hughes replied, fingering the brooch. "My father gave it to me."

Amy nodded. Diana's father gave her lots of pretty trinkets. Amy suspected it was because Diana's mother had left the family, and Mr. Hughes somehow thought giving Diana and her brother, David, presents would help them forget the disgrace. But Amy knew Diana and David would rather have their mother home than any gift their father could possibly offer them.

"It is pretty," Jenny Snow said, walking over to Amy and Diana with her friend Susie Perkins. "Is it gold, Diana?"

"I suppose so," Diana replied. "It didn't occur to me to ask."

Amy grinned. Before Diana's arrival in Concord, Amy had longed to be friends with Jenny and Susie, but they had hardly acknowledged her existence. Now that she and Diana had become friends, Jenny and Susie were always trying to include themselves in their conversations. Amy knew it was because Diana was the only girl in their grade who was prettier and richer than they were. But Diana was also nicer, and Amy cherished her friendship.

"My parents give me gifts all the time," Jenny said. "Of course, a true lady wouldn't think to ask the value of a gift. I simply assumed your father would have told you."

"He merely said the brooch made him think of me on his most recent trip," Diana said.

"I'm sure it is true gold," said Susie. "Mr. Hughes would never buy anything cheap for Diana."

"I know my father never would," Jenny said. "And Mr. Perkins gives Susie the loveliest things."

Amy wished she could say the same of her father. She wasn't even sure he would give her and her sisters gold jewelry if he could afford to. Father seemed to think it was more important to share what little they had than to indulge in selfish pleasures.

"Amy should have pretty things as well," said Diana. "But Mr. March is away doing such noble work with our soldiers. It makes me feel guilty to be taking any enjoyment in this brooch when I think of what our boys are enduring."

"How true," said Jenny.

"I think of our brave soldiers all the time," said Susie.

Amy swallowed a laugh. Jenny and Susie never thought of anyone but themselves.

Not that she was much different. Amy felt a familiar surge of guilt because she wanted pretty jewelry when what she should be wanting was her father's safe return from the war.

"Hello, Amy."

"Oh, hello, Robert," Amy said. She hadn't even noticed Robert Lloyd approaching them. He was a quiet boy her age. She'd known him for years, and for years he had said hello to her before the school day began.

"Good-bye," he said, walking away as quietly as he had walked toward her. The girls watched as he left.

"Robert's sweet on you," Jenny proclaimed.

"Robert loves Amy," Susie chanted.

"Stop it," Amy said. "He's just my friend."

"You have lots of friends," Jenny said. "But they don't look at you the way Robert does."

"There's love in his eyes," said Susie.

"How would you know?" Amy asked. "Do you have many suitors?"

Susie blushed. "Of course not," she said. "True ladies don't have suitors until they're of marriageable age. At least sixteen."

"Older than that," said Jenny. "First you make your debut, and then men pursue you, and then you select the one who offers you the most."

"The most what?" Amy asked.

"The most of what you want," Jenny replied. "My mother explained it all to me. One man might offer you position in society. Another might offer true love. And another might simply have money. If a girl has social position and a pleasing appearance, she can decide what is most important to her and choose the man who most pleases her."

"It's so exciting," said Susie. "I can't wait to be a bride. I should like so much to marry a man with true social standing. He doesn't have to be from Boston. A New Yorker would be acceptable as well."

Amy wished she could be so optimistic about her own chances of marrying into society. But then she glanced at Diana, whose parents had been perfectly suited. Their marriage hadn't lasted anyway.

"I think before we plan our weddings, we should work on our sums," Amy said. "Study our spelling. Memorize our history dates."

Diana smiled. "Learn our capitals," she said. "Practice our penmanship."

"How boring," said Jenny. "I'd rather dream of my wedding day."

"I'm sure we all would," Susie said. "Except maybe for Amy."

"And why shouldn't I dream of my wedding day?" Amy asked, even though she'd just pointed out that it was foolish of them to be doing so.

"I'm sorry, Amy," said Susie. "It's just that a truly beautiful wedding is fiercely expensive. You have three sisters to be married off as well. I'm sure you'll find an upstanding gentleman to marry, Amy. A minister, perhaps, like your father, or a teacher. And your wedding will be charming. Your mother has such lovely taste, and she manages to do so much with so little. It'll be a quiet ceremony in your parlor, no doubt. I only hope there's room enough for your friends to attend as well."

Amy wasn't sure, but she thought she saw Susie smirk. What angered her most was her awareness that Susie was probably right. How could she ever hope to marry a wealthy man of

16

social position when her family had so few means?

The schoolbell rang. "Come, Amy," said Diana. "We have our penmanship to practice."

"And our sums to learn," Amy said. She linked arms with Diana. Now that Beth was taking her lessons at home, Diana was the person Amy spent the most time with at school. And as sweet as Beth was, Diana was far better dressed.

Amy noticed Robert Lloyd walking toward his classroom. "Hello, Robert," she said, smiling.

Robert looked up and smiled back. "Hello, Amy."

As Amy followed Diana into their classroom, she thought about Robert. Could he really be sweet on her? If he was, might he ever want to marry her? The Lloyds were a prosperous family, much respected in Concord. Amy knew she could make a worse match.

Amy caught Diana looking at her and knew Diana was reading her mind.

"All right," Amy murmured. "Penmanship first."

Diana laughed. "The better for writing thank-you notes," she said.

Still, Amy couldn't help thinking that even a small wedding in her parents' parlor would be acceptable if she could only marry the man of her dreams.

And right now, for lack of another choice, Robert Lloyd was the man she dreamed about.

CHAPTER 3

"*H*ow do you get a man to fall in love with you?" Amy asked Meg later that afternoon. The girls were sitting in the parlor. Jo was reading, and Beth was sewing a dress for one of her dolls. Meg was working on her mending, and Amy was pretending to do her schoolwork. Marmee was out helping with war work, and Hannah, the family housekeeper, was in the kitchen. Amy figured this was as good a time as any to bring up the subject of love and marriage.

Meg looked up from her mending. "How should I know?" she asked. "No man has ever fallen in love with me."

"But they will," said Jo, putting her book down. "Meg, you'll have legions of suitors once Marmee allows you to."

"I don't want legions," said Meg. "Just the right one."

"But how do you get that one to fall in love with you?" Amy persisted. "Are there special tricks?"

"Do you think Marmee used special tricks?" Jo asked.

"No, of course not," Amy replied. "Marmee would never resort to trickery. But I'm sure there are little things a girl can do to help a man realize he's in love."

"Amy," Jo said sharply. "You're far too young to be thinking such things."

"Sometimes I think about it," said Beth. "Am I too young?"

"You think about getting a man to fall in love with you?" Amy asked. Somehow she'd assumed Beth thought only about her family, her dolls, and her kittens.

"Sometimes," Beth said. "Jo's plays make

me wonder. Her heroes and heroines are always so deeply in love. Nothing stops them. Not evil curses, or dastardly dukes, or floods, or ghosts. Of course, death stops them sometimes, but you always get the feeling they keep loving each other even after one of them has died."

"This is nothing against Jo's plays," said Meg, "but I'm not sure the plots are that realistic."

"I believe in grand passion," declared Jo. "Father and Marmee have a grand passion. And there's a war now, keeping them apart. The heart of my plays is realistic, even if the events aren't the sort that happen in Concord daily."

"Thank goodness," Meg said. "All those curses and dastardly dukes. Concord has enough going on without them."

"Does it?" Amy asked. "Are you really satisfied with life in Concord, Meg? Don't you wish for something more glamorous?"

"Our little Amy is in a mood," said Jo.

"Making a man fall in love with her isn't enough. She wants to trap some wealthy man who'll offer her the world."

"You want the world too," Amy said.

"I admit I do," said Jo. "But I'll earn it on my own."

"I'm willing to do that," Amy said. "Through my art. But just because I'm going to be an artist doesn't mean I don't want to fall in love."

"That's not what you were saying," Jo answered. "You weren't asking about falling in love. You were asking about how to get a man to fall in love with you."

"All girls have their little tricks," Meg said. "Except perhaps Marmee."

"And Aunt March," Beth said. Her sisters laughed.

"Most girls, then," said Meg. "A lady doesn't use too much artifice, but a little is allowed."

"Dropping your handkerchief," said Jo. "Fluttering your eyelashes."

"Being held prisoner in a tower by a dastardly duke," said Beth. "That always works for Jo's heroines."

"There aren't many towers in Concord," Amy said.

"There aren't many wealthy men in Concord," Meg said. "But there are good men, and that's the sort we should hope to fall in love with."

"Men like Father," said Jo. "We should all be fortunate if we find men as good as he."

Amy knew that was true. She also knew she wanted something more. Or at least different.

"Does dropping your handkerchief really work?" she asked.

Meg laughed. "No man ever fell in love because a girl couldn't hold her handkerchief," she said.

"Even when my heroines are locked in towers, that's not why my heroes fall in love," Jo said. "The damsels are beautiful and good, as well as prisoners."

"So being beautiful *and* good would do it?" Amy asked.

"Good first," said Meg. "Then beautiful."

"Marmee is beautiful because she's good," Beth said. "That's the best sort of beauty."

"But it's not the sort that lands rich husbands," said Jo, much to Amy's relief, since that was what she was thinking.

"Rich men want rich wives," Meg said. "It's not fair, but it's true. Girls like us can never dream of rich husbands."

"Does that mean we'll have poor husbands?" Amy asked.

"No," Meg said. "We're respectable. We'll find respectable husbands. Ministers. Teachers."

Amy's heart sank. She was back to having a simple, tasteful wedding in the parlor.

Jo laughed. "It does sound boring," she said. "Poor Amy. Her heart is set on a duke at the very least. Not a minister. Not a teacher. And if the truth be known, my dreams are a little more daring as well. I'd like a man who resembles one of my heroes. A man who would battle floods and curses to rescue me from the tower. Not that I'm likely ever to be imprisoned in a tower. But that sort of man. A real hero."

"Father is a real hero," Beth said.

Jo nodded. "He is, I agree," she said. "But there are heroes and there are heroes. I'd like the kind who wears a sword and duels to the death for his grand passion."

"Mine doesn't have to duel," said Amy. "But I certainly would like him to have money."

"That's wicked," said Meg. "You would never marry for money, would you, Amy? Even if you had the chance?"

Amy thought of the wealthy men she'd met in Concord, Boston, and New York. They all seemed so old, so stodgy—or, in the case of Diana's father, so unhappy. "No," she said. "But surely there must be one wealthy man out there who is good and kind and handsome and daring and willing to marry a girl with no money."

"Good luck finding him," said Meg.

"And if you do, see if he has a brother," said Jo, and she and her sisters collapsed together in laughter.

CHAPTER 4

"Amy, be a dear and take this book over to Aunt March's," Marmee said as she entered the parlor. "I promised it to her, and I simply don't have the energy to take it myself."

"Did you work that hard, Marmee?" Meg asked as she and her sisters hovered around their mother.

"No harder than any of the other women," Marmee replied. "But there's so much to do if our soldiers aren't to be cold this winter. I simply haven't the energy to deal with Aunt March just now."

"Why can't Jo go?" Amy asked.

"Because Jo sees quite enough of Aunt March, thank you very much," Jo said. "Amy, do what Marmee asks of you, and don't put up a battle."

"I was just asking," Amy muttered, taking the book from her mother. "Do you expect anything from Aunt March in return?"

"Just lectures and scoldings, I'm sure," said Marmee. "Oh, dear. I really shouldn't say such things. I'm afraid I have a headache, girls. Perhaps a little rest will help."

"Then go rest, and don't worry about us," Jo said. "Amy, run off like a good child, and that will be one less thing for Marmee to worry about."

"I'll be back soon," Amy said, but she knew no one really cared. They were fussing over Marmee instead, helping her off with her shoes, massaging her forehead. Amy scooted out the door as Meg ran to the kitchen to fetch a cup of tea.

Amy tried to feel sorry for herself, but she really couldn't. It was natural for Marmee to ask her to carry the book to Aunt March. Meg had recently started work as a governess, and she helped out at home as well. Jo spent every day with Aunt March and could hardly be expected to return there once she'd made her afternoon escape. As for Beth, she froze in terror whenever she was forced to exchange greetings with Aunt March. Marmee would never ask her to go unless it was absolutely necessary.

Besides, Amy was Aunt March's favorite. Amy smiled to herself as she began the short walk. She knew she wasn't supposed to know that, or at least to acknowledge it, but it was true. And she was fond of Aunt March in return. Aunt March was a fierce scold, but she smiled more often than she frowned at Amy.

It was a lovely early autumn afternoon, and Amy enjoyed the walk. It gave her a chance to daydream about her husband. Very rich, very handsome. Very good, as well. Perhaps not as good as Father, but Amy was sure her husband's wealth would help her forget that.

She arrived at Aunt March's in very good

spirits and asked the butler to see whether Aunt March might receive her. The answer was yes, and Amy was led to the back parlor. Amy admired a house with more than one parlor.

"Aunt March," Amy said, walking over to the elderly lady and bending down so that she might be kissed. Aunt March had given no sign that she would get up to greet Amy.

"Amy," Aunt March said. "What's the reason for this pleasant surprise?"

"Marmee asked me to bring this book to you," Amy replied. "She would have come herself, but she was too tired after working all day preparing linens and bandages for our soldiers."

"As good an excuse as any," said Aunt March. "Sit down, child. Let me have a look at you. Do you have enough to eat? Sometimes I worry about you girls and how well you're fed."

"We eat more than enough," Amy said. "Good solid foods."

x

Aunt March laughed. "Good solid foods," she said. "Do I sense you'd care for something a bit more exciting, Amy?"

Amy smiled, glanced down toward the floor, and tried fluttering her eyelashes. "You know me too well, Aunt March," she said.

"I know all my nieces," Aunt March responded. "And I suspect I know what will become of them."

"You do?" Amy asked, unable to keep the excitement from her voice. "Can you really guess at our futures?"

"I'm not a prophet," Aunt March replied. "But I reckon myself a good judge of character. I'm fairly sure I know what lies in store for each of you."

"Oh, tell me, please," Amy said.

"Will you tell your sisters if I do?" Aunt March asked.

"Not if you don't want me to," Amy said.

"Very well." Aunt March was silent for a moment. "Whom shall I start with?"

Amy wanted Aunt March to start with her,

but she knew better than to say so. "Start with Meg," she said. "As the oldest. Then Jo, and Beth, and me. If you've bothered to think of me at all."

"I think a great deal about you," Aunt March said. "But Margaret is as good a place to start as any. She will make a match. Not a dazzling one, but a good one. A respectable man. A widower, I think, an older man with several children. A man who won't need a wealthy wife, but a steady one who will give him happiness in his old age."

Amy thought such a future sounded perfectly dreadful but knew better than to say so. "And Jo," she said. "What will her future be?"

Aunt March shook her head. "Josephine is a scandal waiting to happen," she said. "I fear she'll bring shame to all the Marches."

"How?" Amy asked.

"By writing one of those plays of hers," Aunt March replied. "The theater is no place for a respectable lady. But Josephine does insist. My only hope is she'll write under that dreadful nickname of hers, and people won't realize she's of the gentler sex."

Amy didn't know whether she was relieved or disappointed at the scandal Jo was going to be. Part of her had hoped for dastardly dukes, but she was old enough to know that if one March girl became involved with a wicked man, it would be enough to ruin the chances of all the March girls.

"And what of Beth?" Amy asked.

"She's not meant for marriage, that one," said Aunt March. "But I'm sure she'll be a comfort to your parents in their old age. It helps to have an unmarried daughter who stays with you and tends to your needs. Somehow, I don't see you performing those services, Amy."

"How *do* you see me?" Amy asked.

Aunt March laughed. "You should see the expression on your face," she said. "Tell me, Amy, how do you want me to see your future?"

Amy suspected she could tell Aunt March

the truth but decided not to risk it. "I only want to lead a good life," she said instead. "The sort Marmee and Father live."

"Of course that's what you want," Aunt March said. "And a fine ambition it is. Very well, child. You may go now. Stop in the kitchen and see if there's anything Cook can give you to take home as a special treat for you and your sisters."

Amy rose, disappointment showing on her face. "Is that how you picture me?" she asked. "Leading a good life?"

"Surely that's what you want," Aunt March replied.

"Of course," Amy said. "But I'm sure Jo doesn't want to lead a scandalous one, and that's how you picture her."

Aunt March laughed. "You're the hope of the Marches," she said. "It's a shame you're the youngest and not the firstborn, although I'm sure Margaret will do all right for herself. But you're the one who'll make the great match. You're born for society, Amy, and you'll find your way to it. Proper society, of course, and only if you remember at all times that you are a lady, that the name of March stands for something other than poverty and good deeds."

Amy sat right back down. "That's what I want, Aunt March," she said. "But I don't see how I can achieve it. Rich men don't marry poor girls. I'm sure they don't."

"Some do," Aunt March said. "Of course, the girl must be pure and without a breath of scandal. She must know how to behave in society. She must have all the accomplishments. Do you think you can manage all that?"

"I don't know," Amy admitted. "I'm sure I can be pure. But how can I learn how to behave in society if I'm never in society? And don't accomplishments cost money?"

"Don't worry, my child," Aunt March said. "When the time comes, if I think it a worthwhile investment, I'll see to it you have your chance. But you must prove to me that you can handle it. Use Diana Hughes for an example. That poor child has a terrible scandal hanging over her, yet she is every inch a lady, and some man will be very fortunate to get her."

"Diana is my dearest friend," Amy said. "It will be easy to learn from her."

"Then do," Aunt March said. "Your mother is a fine woman, but she turned her back on wealth and society when she chose to marry my nephew. Learn from her about goodness, and learn from others about society. If you get the balance just right, you'll make a splendid match, and be happy as well. I was happy in my marriage, you know. A successful match does not have to be a loveless one."

"Thank you, Aunt March," Amy said, rising and giving her a kiss. "Sometimes I think I could learn more from you than I ever could from school."

"You're probably right," Aunt March said. "But you'll need your schooling, so pay attention to that as well. Now, go to the kitchen and get that treat, or I'll picture you hungry all evening!"

Amy thanked Aunt March again and made her way to the kitchen. Ordinarily she'd be excited at the prospect of a special treat, but with thoughts of a fine society marriage racing through her head, she had all the treat she needed.

CHAPTER 5

*I*t was still warm enough to sit outside for lunch, so the next day Amy ate under the oak tree with Diana.

"Do you think about your wedding day?" Amy asked as she nibbled in her most ladylike fashion on an apple.

Diana shook her head. "Marriage scares me," she said. "I try not to think about it."

"But weddings aren't the same as marriage," Amy said. "Don't you ever dream of yourself in a grand ballroom, swirling about in a beautiful white gown?"

"It wouldn't matter if I did," Diana said. "The man I marry, if I ever should, would have to want me very much to forgive me for my mother's actions." She spoke so softly, Amy had to strain to hear her. "Such a man would never have money. If Father thinks I simply must be married, he'll find a man willing to have me for my dowry. But the wedding would have to be a quiet one, and I doubt love would enter into the marriage."

"But that's terrible," Amy said, trying to keep her voice to a whisper. She knew how ashamed Diana was of her mother's desertion, and how desperate she was that their schoolmates not find out her secret.

"What's terrible?" Jenny asked, sitting down next to Diana. Naturally, Susie followed.

Diana flashed a look of horror at Amy.

"We were just talking about my wedding day," Amy said, trying to think of something interesting so that Jenny wouldn't suspect the truth. "And Diana was saying I simply shouldn't dream of having a grand society wedding."

"Diana, how mean of you," said Jenny. "Let Amy dream if she wants."

"I spoke to Mama about poor Amy last night," Susie said.

"You did?" Amy asked.

Susie nodded. "My mother thinks your mother is a fine lady," Susie said. "According to Mama, a true lady remains one no matter how poor she might be. Which, of course, your mother is. Mama says it's an absolute necessity that one of the March girls make a fine match, and she supposes you'd have as good a chance as any. But she says you can't simply sit back and wait for it to happen the way Jenny and Diana and I can because of our social position. You'll need a good deal of help if you're to raise your family from the gutter."

"The Marches aren't in the gutter," Diana said as Amy was about to speak up. "And I don't think Amy will need any help at all. She's so pretty and smart and nice, some fine man is bound to fall in love with her."

Jenny laughed. "You're so naive," she said. "Just because a fine man may fall in love with a girl like Amy doesn't mean he'll marry her.

39

Susie and her mother are right. Amy needs all the help we can give her."

"Even if that's true, I'm sure it can wait a few years," said Diana. "Unless you want her to be a child bride."

"Mama says it shouldn't wait," Susie replied. "Marriage is a woman's whole life. Amy should already be thinking about what she must do to find the right husband. She can't afford to make any mistakes."

"No lady can," said Diana.

"Of course not," said Jenny. "Amy even less than the rest of us."

Amy thought of a life without mistakes. Of a life led perfectly. Even if such a life meant marrying an incredibly rich duke who adored her, and whom she adored back, it sounded like more work than it was worth. "I think I'd rather have some fun first," she said. "Paint my pictures. Play games. Learn my sums."

"You say that now," Susie replied. "But in ten years, when no man of any social standing will have you, you'll be sorry."

"I'm sorry now to be listening to such rubbish," Diana declared, getting up and brushing her skirt off. "Amy, I'll be inside, if you want to continue our conversation."

"In a moment," Amy said. She was angry that Susie had said her family was in the gutter, but she was strangely glad that Mrs. Perkins had bothered to consider her future. It had been exciting enough when Aunt March had talked about it, but Aunt March was family. Mrs. Perkins was not.

"What you need is practice," Jenny said once Diana had left them. "Don't you agree, Susie?"

"Absolutely," Susie replied. "It's all well and good to lead a flawless life, but if a man doesn't notice you in the first place, what difference will it make if you're pure and good?"

Jenny nodded. "You have breeding," she said to Amy. "But no money. Of course, breeding is better than money, but money really is a help."

"That's why you need practice," Susie said. "The sooner, the better."

41

"Hello, Amy."

"Oh, hello, Robert," Amy said, looking up at the sound of his voice. "It's a very nice day, isn't it?"

"Uh, yes," Robert said. Amy could see how uncomfortable he was speaking with her while she sat with Jenny and Susie. She smiled at him as he ran off to join the other boys.

"Robert would be perfect for you to practice on," said Jenny. "He's sweet on you anyway, Amy, so he'd be certain to enjoy any attentions you gave him."

"He's from a fine family, too," Susie said. "The Lloyds are very respectable people. He might even marry you, Amy, if he loves you enough."

Jenny nodded. "I'm sure he's the best you could hope for," she said. "His family might not approve at first, but if Robert's been in love with you since childhood, he'd insist, and wear them down. Mother's told me of many such marriages."

"I say he's in love with you already!" Susie cried. "Oh, Amy, how wonderful for you, to land a boy like Robert Lloyd. I'm sure Mama would approve."

Amy thought about Aunt March. She knew and liked the Lloyds, who certainly had wealth and social position. Robert might not be a duke, but then again, Amy wouldn't have to be perfect all the time to catch him.

And Robert would have no illusions about the Marches. He'd seen Jo in her rough-and-tumble play. He knew how shy Beth was, and how poor the Marches were. Amy was sure her friends were right, and that he was sweet on her. He certainly took every opportunity to say hello to her.

"I like Robert," she admitted. "He's quite nice."

"Yes, he is," said Jenny. "He'll make a good husband. So you must start now, Amy, or else you'll lose your chance at him and he'll marry someone like Diana instead."

"Diana?" Amy asked.

"A girl with breeding and money," Susie said. "The kind of girl I'm sure the Lloyds expect Robert to marry."

"But not if you capture his heart," Jenny insisted. "Which you simply must do, Amy March, if you're to have any chance at a happy life."

Amy wasn't certain that was true. But Aunt March and Mrs. Perkins both seemed to feel that Amy should begin to prepare herself if she wanted a society marriage. And surely they knew more than Amy did about such matters.

Still, that didn't mean she had to let Jenny and Susie know of her plans. It was satisfying enough that they talked about her, but Amy suspected Jo and Beth talked about her too, and she didn't want them planning her future.

"I'm sure I'm too young to worry about such things," she said, standing up with as much dignity as she could muster. "If I'm meant for a society marriage, then it will happen. If not, just as long as I marry a man good and true, I know I'll find real happiness."

Susie shook her head. "Not according to Mama, you won't," she said, but Amy pretended not to hear her. Still, as she walked back toward the school, she made a point of strolling in Robert's direction. She was pleased to see him look up at her, and she smiled right at him.

"Hello, Robert," she said.

"Hello, Amy," he said, blushing furiously.

Amy smiled. Getting Robert Lloyd to fall in love with her might be just as simple as Jenny and Susie had said.

CHAPTER 6

*E*ven though Amy had decided to capture Robert's heart, and had thought of little else while working on her sums and penmanship that afternoon, she was still surprised to see him lingering in the yard after school.

"Hello, Robert," Amy said, as she'd said a thousand times before.

"Hello, Amy. I was wondering if I could walk you home today."

"I'd like that." Amy shifted her schoolbooks on her arm and was delighted when Robert gestured to show her that he would carry them for her. Her smile was broad and genuine, and

Robert smiled right back. One of his teeth was chipped. Amy had never noticed this before, and wondered if the tooth could be pulled and a false one put in someday.

The two of them walked silently toward the March house. Amy wasn't accustomed to such a quiet walk. Even when she and Beth had been the only ones heading home from school, they'd had much to chatter about. She considered dropping her handkerchief, but it was her best one and she couldn't risk its getting dirty. Besides, Robert's arms were filled with her schoolbooks. Instead she fluttered her lashes.

"Is something the matter?" Robert asked. "Did you get a cinder in your eyes?"

"Yes," Amy said. "I mean no. I mean, I don't know. My lashes just got fluttery. That happens with girls sometimes."

"Oh," Robert said.

Amy wished she understood eyelash fluttering better. Perhaps that was one of the accomplishments Aunt March thought she should have. Still, conversation had proved better than silence, so Amy searched for another topic.

"Isn't this a lovely fall?" she said. "I don't recall ever seeing a prettier one."

"It is nice, I guess," said Robert. "Sometimes I wish I weren't in school, the weather's so nice."

"Oh, I know just what you mean!" Amy exclaimed. "Today I would have loved to be out, taking a walk in the garden."

"I'd rather be hunting," said Robert. "In the woods, looking for game."

Father didn't hunt. And Amy, who loved meat, tried very hard never to think of just where it came from. "I've never been hunting," she said. "But today does seem to be just the perfect day for it."

Robert smiled, so Amy supposed she'd said the right thing. "My father says hunting is fine sport," Robert told her. "Of course the sport right now would be to hunt some of those Johnny Rebs."

"My father's with the Union Army," Amy

said. "Of course he isn't a soldier. He's a chaplain for our soldiers. But that's very dangerous work as well." She felt a surge of guilt that she was bragging about the danger Father was in. Still, it was for his own good. She was only planning to marry this chipped-toothed, gun-toting boy for Father and Marmee's sake.

"An army needs chaplains," said Robert. "But it needs arms and men who know how to use them even more. That's what my father says."

"You have an older brother," Amy said. "He's older than Meg even. Will he be joining the army?"

"He wants to," Robert replied. "My father's dead set against it, though. Says none of his sons are going to die just to free some slaves."

"Oh," said Amy.

Robert looked over at her. "That's just what my father says," he said. "A boy should respect his father, but he doesn't have to agree. If the war's still going in a year or two, I just might join up myself. Maybe your father will be chaplain to me someday."

"Oh, Robert," said Amy. "You'd be so young and in so much danger."

"There's drummer boys my age," said Robert. "On both sides, I suspect. No one's going to say Johnny Reb's braver than I am."

"I never would," Amy responded. "I think you're quite the bravest boy I've ever met."

Robert grinned, and Amy smiled. Talking to Robert wasn't all that different from talking to Aunt March, she realized. In both cases, all she needed to do was keep saying what they wanted to hear.

She had a quick image of a life in which she always said the right thing, always tried to please. She pictured Robert as old as Aunt March and looking somewhat like her, only with a chipped tooth. It was a dreadful thought. Amy was used to speaking her mind. For one quick moment, she felt a flash of genuine sympathy for Jo, having to spend all her days watching her tongue with Aunt March around. But then Amy focused on the task at hand.

"Do you think the war will last two years?"

she asked Robert. "I should hate it so if Father stayed away that long."

Robert shook his head. "We'll have those rebs licked in no time," he declared. "Your father will be home by Christmas."

"That's what I pray for," Amy said. "We miss him terribly."

"War's good for a man," said Robert. "But it's hard on the women."

"It's hard on us," Amy said. "I know that to be true."

"That's your house up ahead, isn't it?" Robert said as the March house came into view.

"It is," Amy replied. "I've had such a good time talking with you, Robert, I didn't realize how far we'd walked."

"I guess I'll stop here then, and go on my way," he said. He dumped Amy's schoolbooks into her arms. "See you tomorrow, I guess."

"I guess," said Amy. She watched as Robert ran off. Boys were so strange, she thought. But maybe he hadn't accompanied her all the way home because he feared she would invite him in for cider and cake and he didn't want to take food from their mouths.

Amy decided it was sweet of Robert to be worrying about her family so. He really was nice, even if he did like to hunt *and* had a chipped tooth.

Amy laughed. It felt good to know she could make a boy like her. She hugged her school-books and skipped the rest of the way home.

CHAPTER 7

*A*my told no one that Robert had walked her home. She suspected her sisters would only tease her, and that Marmee might not approve. She didn't plan on telling any school friends, either. Diana would shake her head, and Jenny and Susie would gloat. It was best kept a secret.

Besides, Amy liked being the only one who knew. As she fell asleep that night, she thought more about Robert. He became better-looking in her mind, more grown-up, less chipped-toothed. She pictured the two of them at a fancy ball, gliding together to a waltz.

"What a handsome couple," people were murmuring just as she fell asleep.

The next morning Amy woke up humming and smiling. No one seemed to notice, which was fine with her.

At school, she forced herself to concentrate on her work. Jenny and Susie might be right about the Lloyds wanting their son to marry better. She owed it to them to have a good education, if not all the accomplishments. Briefly, she wondered how much accomplishments cost, and how willing Aunt March would be to pay for some. But then she stopped dreaming and started listening as her teacher lectured about Christopher Columbus.

It was hard, though, thinking about schoolwork and not wondering whether Robert would walk her home again. Amy wished the two of them were in the same class. It would help if she could actually look at him and his chipped tooth, and remind herself of his less than perfect ways. But he was nowhere to be seen, and her mind filled with images of them waltzing together.

Diana chose to have lunch indoors, and Amy joined her. Since Amy didn't dare tell her the most important thing that had ever happened to her, she didn't have much to say. Diana did most of the talking, relating stories about her brother, David, who attended boarding school.

"You're so lucky," said Jenny as she and Susie joined them.

"Why is that?" asked Diana.

"Well, when David comes home for visits, he must bring back the most wonderful boys for you to meet," said Jenny.

"I wish I had an older brother," said Susie. "Mama says they're simply the best asset a girl can have."

"David just began boarding school this year," replied Diana. "He might never bring a friend home."

"Why shouldn't he?" Jenny asked. "Your home is so beautiful, Diana. I'm sure he'd want to show it off."

Amy knew why Diana had her doubts.

David was sensitive about his mother not living with his father and probably wouldn't care to make further explanations. She knew Jenny had seen Diana's house not by invitation, but because she'd chosen to drop by one day and Diana had had no choice but to show her around.

Amy glanced at Jenny and Susie. She had longed once for their friendships, but now that she knew them, they seemed petty and ambitious, and she hardly liked them at all.

"David's a very nice boy," she said. "I'm sure his friends will be every bit as nice. Perhaps one day your father will take you to visit David at school, Diana."

Diana smiled. "I'd like that. I do miss him."

"I can't imagine what life would be like without my sisters," said Amy. "Quieter, I suppose, but not nearly as much fun."

"How does Meg like her work?" Diana asked. "I think of her often. And Jo? Does she get along with Mrs. March?"

Jenny tilted her head, clearly a signal to Susie. "We'll let you two discuss Amy's family now," she said. "Susie and I have other things to talk about. Don't we, Susie?"

"We do?" Susie asked. "Oh, I'm sure we must. Very well, Jenny." She followed her friend, as she always did, a step or two behind.

Amy and Diana laughed. "I know of no better way to rid myself of them," Diana said.

"You mean you don't want to know how Meg and Jo are doing?" Amy asked.

Diana looked stricken. "Of course I do," she said. "That's just such a fine way to kill two birds with one stone."

"I'll tell them you said so," replied Amy, and began relating to Diana all Meg's and Jo's adventures.

After lunch, Amy found it much easier to practice her penmanship and do her sums. Robert seemed suddenly unimportant. Somewhere, she was sure, was the man she would waltz with. But he didn't have to be Robert. Robert was Jenny and Susie's choice for her, and Jenny and Susie were silly, bossy girls.

Still, Amy was pleased when she saw Robert

waiting for her at the end of the school day. "Hello," she said.

"I was wondering if I could walk you home," he said.

"I'd like that," Amy replied. After all, she didn't have to marry him to enjoy his company.

"I was thinking about what we talked about yesterday," Robert said, as they approached the village square.

"What was that?" Amy asked.

"About the war and all," he said. "I liked talking to you. Say, isn't that your sister over there?"

"Where?" Amy asked. She looked where Robert was pointing but saw none of her sisters.

"I thought I saw Beth," Robert said. "She must have just gone into one of the shops. I like her. She's quiet."

"That she is," Amy agreed. She grimaced. *Oh, dear,* she thought. *Am I supposed to be quiet?* But then she remembered she no longer intended to marry Robert and didn't care.

"Wait a second," Robert said. He put down his schoolbooks and Amy's on a park bench. Amy squinted against the bright sunlight. She hoped Robert wouldn't ask about her fluttery eyes again.

"This is for you," he said, pulling something from his trouser pocket.

"Why, thank you," Amy said.

Robert handed her the object. "I don't know," he said. "I thought maybe you'd like it." He picked up the schoolbooks and began walking.

Amy scurried to catch up with him, looking curiously at what he had given her. It was a gold locket, with lots of pretty stones.

"It's lovely," she said. "It's quite the prettiest piece of jewelry I've ever seen."

"I'm glad you like it," Robert said. "It doesn't mean anything, of course. Just a locket. You don't have to wear it if you don't want to."

"Of course I want to," said Amy. "I love jewelry. Wait a moment, Robert, while I put it on."

Robert stood still and watched as Amy fastened the chain of the locket around her neck. Amy couldn't wait to get home and examine it in the mirror.

"What a nice thing for you to do," she said. "I'll cherish this locket always."

Robert smiled. His chipped tooth suddenly didn't look nearly so bad.

Amy thought about kissing him on the cheek but decided that would be too forward of her. She smiled back at him instead. "No one's ever given me such a pretty gift," she said. "Thank you, Robert, so very much."

"You're welcome," he said. "The stones are blue, like your eyes. I thought it would look pretty on you."

"I'll wear it always," Amy said.

"Maybe you shouldn't do that," Robert said. "Not to school. You know how girls talk."

Amy knew just how girls talked. "You're right," she said. "I'll keep it to myself for a while. It'll be my special secret."

Robert looked relieved. But Amy didn't

care. He was no longer the dashing gentleman she imagined waltzing with, but he was a boy who liked her enough to notice the color of her eyes, and for the moment, that was all that she needed to make her happy.

CHAPTER 8

obert left Amy, as he had the day before, not quite at her doorstep. Amy didn't mind. She was eager to see what the locket looked like on her.

She raced upstairs and found the mirror on Meg's dresser. She held it just far enough away to examine the locket. The blue of the stones almost matched the blue of her eyes. Amy had never seen anything quite so pretty. She only hoped that if she didn't marry Robert, she'd still be allowed to keep it.

"What are you fussing over?" Jo asked, entering the room, which she shared with Meg.

Amy turned and nearly dropped the mirror.

"Be careful!" Jo cried. "Seven years' bad luck, and Meg's wrath forever."

"I'm sorry," Amy said. She hadn't expected Jo to come in. Much to her horror, Meg followed almost immediately. Even Beth seemed to materialize from the shadows.

Amy felt guilty of some terrible crime, although all she had been doing was looking in the mirror. "I'll go now," she said. "I'm sorry to have bothered your things, Meg."

"The mirror's as much yours as mine," said Meg. "You know you can use it whenever you want."

"Christopher Columbus," said Jo.

"Don't use slang," Meg said. "Oh, my, Amy. Is that what you were admiring?"

"What?" Amy asked. "Is there something the matter?"

"I don't know," said Meg. "That locket around your neck. Wherever did you get it?"

"Diana gave it to me," Amy said, startling herself with the speed and the depth of her falsehood. "Today. At school."

Jo whistled, which ordinarily would have set Meg off on a lecture about ladylike manners. But Meg seemed too startled to scold Jo.

"Take it off," she said instead. "Let me look at it, Amy."

Amy obeyed. She handed the locket over to Meg.

"Do you think those stones are real?" Jo asked as she hovered by Meg's side. Only Beth seemed uninterested.

"I don't know," Meg said. "I've never really looked at a fine piece of jewelry before."

"I'm sure they're not," said Amy. "Diana's father gives her trinkets all the time."

"This is no trinket," Jo said. "Aunt March has a pin with stones like this one. I asked her about it once, and she said they were sapphires and very valuable and unless I greatly changed my ways, she doubted I'd ever be worthy of them." Jo laughed. "To think my baby sister has already gotten some."

"Oh, but she can't keep them," said Meg. "Not if they have value. Amy, you'll simply have to give the locket back to Diana tomorrow."

"No!" said Amy. "Why should I? Diana knew what she was giving away." Amy suddenly felt so righteous, she almost forgot Diana had nothing to do with the locket.

"But didn't you inquire whether the locket had value?" Meg asked. "You must have wondered."

"Would you have asked?" Amy replied. "That wouldn't have been very ladylike."

"No, I suppose not," said Meg. "Still, you shouldn't accept such expensive gifts."

"And why not?" Amy demanded. "Diana and I are dear friends. She was the one who wanted me to have the locket. I never asked for it. Besides, we don't know that the locket has value. The blue stones could be colored glass. Jo wouldn't recognize the difference, and you just said yourself, Meg, that you don't know."

"I suppose that's true," Meg said. "There's no harm in one friend giving another a little present. It's just that we have nothing to give in return."

"Diana isn't expecting anything," Amy said. "Our friendship is gift enough for her."

"You are right about that," said Meg. "Poor child. Very well. If Marmee says you may keep the locket, I suppose there's no reason why you shouldn't."

"I still say those are real sapphires," Jo insisted. "Perhaps we should show the locket to Aunt March and get her opinion."

"No!" said Amy and Beth at the exact same time.

Jo laughed. "I understand why Amy wants to keep the locket a secret," she said. "But why should you care, Bethy?"

"I don't," Beth said. "I just don't see why Aunt March needs to become involved."

"I don't either," Meg said. She gave the locket back to Amy. "Do show it to Marmee, though. She might know if the sapphires are real, and she'll certainly know whether you should keep it."

"I will." Amy carried the locket to her bedroom. She felt bad about having lied to her sisters, and so easily at that. She dreaded even more lying to Marmee. But Amy was certain Marmee would make her return the locket if she knew Robert had given it to her. And whether they were real sapphires or not, Amy liked owning a locket that matched her eyes.

But Marmee didn't come home until after supper, and when she did, it was clear to her daughters that she was too exhausted to talk.

"We need so much more," Marmee said. "More cloth, more workers, more money. This dreaded war has only just begun, and already I fear for our soldiers. If I were younger and didn't have you girls, I'd work as a nurse."

"Do you think I should do that?" asked Meg.

Marmee shook her head. "You're a dear girl," she said. "Your heart is in the right place. But you're far too young for the brutality you would see. Stay here and be a comfort to me. To your father, too. I received a letter from him today."

"Did you, Marmee?" Jo said. "What does he write?"

The girls gathered around their mother as she sat by the parlor fire. "He thinks of all of you," Marmee said. "Much of the letter is about the work he is doing, the suffering of our soldiers, and of the rebel soldiers as well. They're all God's children, and it grieves him that their blood must be shed, even for so righteous a cause. Here. Let me read the part about you girls."

"Yes, do, Marmee," Meg said. "I miss Father so, and any words from him will make it seem as though he were here with us."

"That's just how I feel," Marmee replied. "Ah, here it is. 'Tell my little women how much I love them and miss them. I think of them at all times, and remember them in my prayers. When my spirits are low, I take the photograph of them out and look into their faces. The fellows here are so used to seeing that picture, they feel as though they know my dear Meg, Jo, Beth, and Amy as well as I do. In some way, my daughters have become their sisters, especially those lads not fortunate enough to have photographs of their own beloved kin. Our cause is a just one, and in many ways we are one family, working and suffering together as one.' "

"I feel so useless," said Jo. "Is there nothing I can do, Marmee, to help our cause?"

"You're help enough to me," said Marmee. "And Father is so proud of you, working to help support us. You too, Meg. Right now, your place is here in Concord. If this dreadful war continues, perhaps then your plans should change. But let's pray for its quick conclusion and Father's safe return home."

"That's what we all pray for," said Jo.

"Day and night," said Beth.

Marmee smiled. "Our prayers will be heeded," she said. "God will not allow slavery to continue in this great country. I'm sure of it. I'm also sure that I'm deathly tired and want nothing more than a kiss good night from each of you and a few hours of dreamless sleep."

"Then that's what you will have," said Jo.

As Amy kissed her mother, she remembered the locket, and how important it had seemed only a few hours before. What did it matter, compared to the suffering her parents were now enduring?

CHAPTER 9

*T*he girls went to bed shortly after Marmee. Amy snuggled under her blanket and thought of the handsome man who had waltzed with her. What was his name? she wondered. When would she meet him?

But Beth interrupted her lovely fantasies. "Why did you lie about the locket?" she asked.

"What?" Amy said, shocked both by the question and by Beth's tone.

"You lied about the locket," Beth said. "I saw Robert Lloyd give it to you in the town square today. Why did you tell Meg and Jo that Diana had given it to you?"

"I don't know," Amy said. "The lie just came out of me. I didn't mean to."

"But you kept on with it," said Beth.

"That's how it is with a lie," Amy replied. "Once you start, you can't just stop and tell the truth instead. And I didn't lie to Marmee. Only to Meg and Jo."

"And me," said Beth.

"But it wasn't a lie to you, because you knew the truth," Amy said. "Only Meg and Jo were deceived. I'm sure they've deceived me in the past, only I haven't known, because they never told the truth."

"It's wrong to lie," Beth said. "I doubt that Meg and Jo ever have, and the only reason you didn't lie to Marmee is because you didn't have the chance. And you lied in the first place because you knew it was wrong to accept the locket from Robert and you were ashamed. You're going to have to give the locket back, and then you'll have to tell Meg and Jo the truth."

Amy sat up in her bed. "No, I don't," she

said. "And I don't like it when you talk to me that way, Beth. It doesn't matter who gave me the locket. What does it matter if it was Robert and not Diana? Perhaps I lied because I didn't want Meg and Jo talking to me the way you just did. Just because you're all older than I am, you think you can boss me around and tell me what's right and what's wrong. Well, you can't. Robert gave me the locket because he likes me and because the color of the stones matches the color of my eyes. It was sweet of him to think of me, and I intend to keep the locket. Someday I'll be all grown up, and lots of men will give me such gifts. That's what happens to pretty girls. And I'll marry one of them, and he'll give me everything I want. Maybe that's not what you want for yourself, but I'm not you, and I wouldn't ever want to be."

Beth was silent. Amy knew her words were hurtful, but she also knew she could have said worse. She thought of Aunt March's prophecy for Beth and congratulated herself on not having revealed it.

"Sometimes you can be a very silly goose," Beth said, sounding just like Jo.

"And sometimes you can be a little prig," Amy replied.

Beth turned her back to Amy. The sisters had had their share of quarrels over the years, and Amy knew that this was Beth's way of saying the discussion had ended. That was fine with Amy. She was more determined than ever to keep the locket. She even hoped the sapphires were real. Beth would have to say she was sorry if Amy ever did marry Robert Lloyd. Which Amy just might do, especially if he got his tooth fixed.

She woke up the next morning before Beth and put the locket in her dresser drawer. Then she dressed quickly, went downstairs, had breakfast, and kept mostly quiet as her sisters and Marmee made their own preparations for the day.

At school Amy looked around for Robert but couldn't find him. She was glad, since that meant it would have been impossible to return the locket to him even if she'd intended to. She made herself think about schoolwork instead and found it surprisingly pleasant to study geography and English rather than imagining herself at a fancy ball.

At lunch Amy and Diana discussed their plans for the weekend. Diana's father had given permission for Amy to spend Saturday night at the Hughes house, and the girls chattered about the upcoming visit. Jenny and Susie tried to join in the conversation, but since they weren't invited, they wandered away soon enough.

As she walked home, Amy delighted in the weather and in the plans for the weekend. Mr. Hughes owned a splendid coach and beautiful horses, and Diana had assured her they could go for a ride Saturday afternoon. Riding in a coach was practically Amy's favorite thing to do, especially when a liveried servant did the driving.

With a start, Amy realized how pleasant it was to walk home by herself and not have to worry about what to say to Robert, and what not to say. Even her schoolbooks felt light.

She laughed at how silly she'd been to ever think of marrying Robert Lloyd, of marrying anybody. She had years to go before she needed to worry about getting a husband.

"There she is now," Amy heard Marmee say as she opened the door. "Amy, come into the parlor immediately."

"What's the matter, Marmee?" Amy cried. "Is it news about Father?"

"No, no," said Marmee. "Amy, this is Mrs. Lloyd. She says you know her son, Robert."

"Of course I do," Amy said. She put her schoolbooks down and curtsyed as she would for Aunt March. "Robert and I go to school together. But he wasn't there today. I hope he isn't ill."

"He's home, being punished," Mrs. Lloyd replied. She didn't look anything like her son. Amy realized she would have felt better if Mrs. Lloyd had had a chipped tooth.

"Amy, Mrs. Lloyd says you have a locket that belongs to her," Marmee declared. "A valuable locket, with real sapphires."

"So they are real!" Amy said, quickly covering her mouth with her hand.

"I take it you have seen the locket," Marmee said.

"Robert gave it to me yesterday," Amy said. "It's in my dresser drawer for safekeeping."

"Robert says you took the locket," said Mrs. Lloyd. "He says you came to our house yesterday afternoon, when I was out paying calls, and took that locket right out of my jewelry case."

"That's a lie," Amy said. "I've never been to your home, Mrs. Lloyd. I would never steal your jewelry."

"Why don't you get the locket?" said Marmee. "I'm sure we can settle all this once Mrs. Lloyd has her locket back."

Amy raced up the stairs. She found Beth sitting on her bed, quietly reading.

"Beth, you have to come downstairs with me," Amy said. "Robert's mother is in the parlor. Please tell her that Robert gave me the locket."

"Oh, Amy," Beth said. "You know how I hate talking to strangers."

"Beth, if you don't, I don't know what will become of me," Amy said. "Mrs. Lloyd thinks I stole her locket. I might even go to jail."

"Mrs. Lloyd might not believe me," Beth said.

"Marmee will." Amy suddenly knew that was the important thing. "Marmee knows you don't lie."

"She should know the same about you," said Beth.

Amy went to her dresser drawer and took out the locket. The sapphires were dazzling in the late-afternoon light. Amy loved knowing that they were real. Perhaps someday someone would give her such a valuable gift.

"Beth, please," she said.

"Couldn't I just tell Marmee after Mrs. Lloyd leaves?" Beth pleaded.

Amy looked at her older sister, saw the real terror in her eyes, and thought about how she'd called her a prig the night before. Beth owed her nothing.

"If that's what you want," Amy said. "It doesn't matter."

She walked downstairs, feeling like one of the heroines in Jo's plays, doomed by a fatal curse. If she was going to die, she might as well make her final exit with grace.

"Here it is," she said as she handed the locket over to Mrs. Lloyd. "I'm sorry for the misunderstanding. I knew it was too beautiful to keep, but Robert told me he wanted me to have it because the stones matched my eyes."

Mrs. Lloyd snatched the locket from Amy. "Keep away from my son, you little hussy," she said. "I never want to see you near him again."

"Very well, Mrs. Lloyd," Marmee said. "You have what you came for. You may now leave."

"With pleasure," Mrs. Lloyd answered. "Good day, Mrs. March."

"Mrs. Lloyd," Marmee said, showing her to the door. "Now, Amy," she said, once Mrs. Lloyd was halfway down the block.

"Would you care to tell me what this was all about?"

"Robert gave me the locket," Amy said, and a tear rolled down her cheek. "Honestly, he did, Marmee. Beth saw him. She can tell you. I never would have stolen it. I would never steal anything."

"Robert did give her the locket," Beth said, coming down the stairs. "I'm sorry, Marmee. I should have told Mrs. Lloyd. If you want, I'll write and tell her. Robert gave Amy the locket in the square yesterday. Hannah sent me to get some flour and beans, and I saw the whole thing."

"Robert noticed you," Amy said. "He mentioned it at the time."

"Then I'm sure we'll be able to clear the matter up," Marmee said. "What I don't understand, Amy, is why you accepted such a valuable present from a boy. And why didn't you ask my permission once Robert had given it to you?"

Amy began crying in earnest. "I was supposed to," she sobbed. "I knew I was doing something wrong. I'm sorry, Marmee. Bethy, I'm sorry."

"Sorry about what?" asked Jo as she entered the house. "What's this scene all about? Does it have to do with that locket Diana gave you?"

"What locket is that?" Marmee asked. Amy was crying too hard to answer.

"Pretty thing," Jo said, flinging off her cape. "Looked like real sapphires to me. Meg and I had quite a discussion about it last night, before we fell asleep. Whether Amy should keep it, whether the stones were real."

"The locket wasn't from Diana," Marmee said. "It was from a boy named Robert Lloyd."

"Christopher Columbus," Jo said. "Why, Amy. You *are* a wicked girl." But instead of looking angry, she laughed.

"I really fail to see the humor in any of this," Marmee said. "Amy, when you're through with your cry, I want to see you in my room.

Wash your face with cold water. I'm not in the mood for more tears."

"Yes, Marmee," Amy mumbled. The only problem was, she didn't know if she'd ever be able to stop crying.

CHAPTER 10

" I'm sorry about everything, Marmee," Amy said a good twenty minutes later. It had taken her that long to be sure no more tears would fall. During that time, Meg had arrived home, and Jo and Beth had filled her in on the story. Meg had been far more disapproving than Jo, and that had only made Amy cry harder.

"You have a great deal to be sorry about," Marmee replied. "Let's start with why Robert gave you the locket. Did you ask him for it?"

"No, of course not," Amy said. "I'd never seen it or heard about it. He just gave it to me. He walked me home from school two days ago, and then yesterday also, and that's when he gave me the locket. It was so pretty, Marmee. I didn't know it was valuable. Was I wrong to accept it?"

"Yes," Marmee said. "Valuable or not, you're too young to be receiving gifts from a boy. A really respectable girl never accepts gifts of jewelry from any man she's not engaged to."

"I didn't know that," Amy said. "I thought girls got lots of gifts and you got to keep them all."

"Not if you want your reputation to remain unblemished," Marmee said. "And for a girl such as you, Amy—pretty, from a respectable but impoverished family—nothing is more important than an unblemished reputation."

"I'm sorry," Amy said. "I didn't know."

"Apparently not," Marmee said. "Frankly, I don't understand why such things should even be of concern to a girl your age. You didn't flirt with Robert, did you, Amy? You didn't lead him on in any way?"

"I don't know," Amy said. "I think I tried, but he didn't seem to understand."

Marmee shook her head. "Perhaps it's my fault," she said. "With your father away, I'm spending so little time at home these days. Perhaps I'm letting you run wild."

"Oh, no, Marmee," Amy said. "It's not your fault. It's just that I want so to marry well, and everybody says I should, and I just thought maybe Robert is the boy I should marry. He likes me."

"Come here, Amy," Marmee said, and Amy sat by her mother's side. "Amy, dearest, you are a very practical girl. Sometimes I think you're the most sensible of all my daughters, even more sensible than Meg. Because of that, I never worry about your future. I know you like pretty things. I know you wish we had more money. But because you're practical and sensible, I know you'll find the right man to marry. And when you do, you'll know there's more to a marriage than being given pretty things by a well-to-do gentleman. You'll know you won't be happy unless there's love on both sides."

"Really?" Amy asked. "You really know that about me?"

Marmee nodded. "I also know you have a conscience. That's why you lied, because you knew what you had done was wrong."

"I did one wrong to hide another," Amy said.

"That's exactly what you did," Marmee replied. "What do you think is the just punishment?"

Amy hated punishments. She swallowed hard as she considered her answer. "I have to write to Mrs. Lloyd and apologize for keeping her locket," she said. "And I have to apologize to Meg and Jo and Beth for lying to them."

"That's a good start," Marmee said.

"I should apologize to you, too," Amy said. "For putting you in that awful position with Mrs. Lloyd. I truly am sorry, Marmee. Do you think I should apologize to Father also?"

"No, that's not necessary," Marmee said. "Do you think apologizing is enough?"

"I suppose not," Amy said with a sigh. "Perhaps I shouldn't go to Diana's house this weekend, even though I was so looking forward to it. I could work with you instead tomorrow, helping our soldiers. That's a good idea, isn't it, Marmee?"

"It's a very good idea," Marmee said, kissing Amy on the forehead.

There was a knock on the door. Meg, Jo, and Beth entered.

"We've been talking," Jo said. "And we think we might have been somewhat responsible for all this, Marmee."

"We've all been dreaming about our future husbands," Meg explained. "I think we put ideas in Amy's head."

"And I know I should have told Mrs. Lloyd the truth," Beth said. "I'll go with you tomorrow, Marmee, if you want, and tell her what I saw."

"Oh, girls," Marmee said. "We're none of us perfect, are we?"

"You are," Amy said.

Marmee shook her head. "Far from it. But

we have each other, and we have our dreams. Maybe that's all we can really hope for."

Amy looked at her mother and her sisters. They did all have their dreams. Dreams of Father's safe return, of a quick and righteous ending to the war. Dreams of husbands and children, of fame and fortune. Dreams of a quiet life, undisturbed by strangers. Dreams of wealth, and beauty, and always of love.

Amy smiled. Someday, she thought, she'd have everything she wanted. But for now, her dreams were the best gift of all.

PORTRAITS OF LITTLE WOMEN ACTIVITIES

FRENCH TOAST

*There's no better way to start the day than with a
plateful of mouthwatering French toast.*

INGREDIENTS
butter to coat the skillet
2 large eggs
½ cup whole milk or half-and-half
1 tablespoon sugar
¼ teaspoon ground nutmeg
1 teaspoon melted butter
2 slices of bread per person (white, raisin,
   challah, or French)

1. Coat a nonstick 12-inch skillet with butter and warm over moderate heat.
2. Mix the eggs and milk in a wide, deep bowl.
3. Add the sugar, nutmeg, and melted butter.
4. Dip each piece of bread into the egg mixture until saturated.
5. Place the bread in the heated pan and lightly brown on each side.
6. Serve each person 2 slices.

French toast is delicious when drizzled with maple syrup or served with jam or jelly, but it's also excellent simply sprinkled with a light coating of powdered sugar.

BEADED NECKLACE AND BRACELET

Beaded jewelry is a wonderful way of expressing your personality. Whether you choose beads that are clear, colored, or frosted, and round, oval, or rectangular, you'll find countless ways of creating beautiful designs.

MATERIALS

Nylon-coated wire (2 inches longer than the desired length of your necklace or bracelet)

2 crimps for each item (available at a craft store)

1 set of clasps for each item (available at a craft store)

Pliers

Beads of your choice (available at a craft store)

Wire cutters

1. Once you've decided on the length of your necklace or bracelet, thread a crimp onto one end of the wire. Place it about ³/₄ inch from the end.
2. Insert half of the clasp through the wire and fold the wire into the crimp.
3. To secure the crimp on the wire, squeeze with the pliers.
4. Thread the beads on the wire. Make sure to leave 1¹/₄ inch of the wire at each end.
5. Thread the remaining wire through the

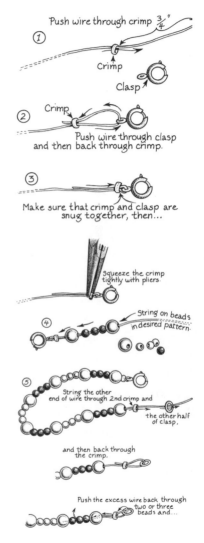

① Push wire through crimp ³/₄"
Crimp
Clasp

② Crimp
Push wire through clasp and then back through crimp.

③ Make sure that crimp and clasp are snug together, then...

Squeeze the crimp tightly with pliers.

④ String on beads in desired pattern.

⑤ String the other end of wire through 2nd crimp and the other half of clasp,

and then back through the crimp.

Push the excess wire back through two or three beads and...

98

second crimp, insert the other half of the clasp, and fold the wire into the crimp and through the last two or three beads. Pull tightly, making sure there is no loose area between the beads, crimp, and clasp. Squeeze the crimp with the pliers. Use the wire cutters to snip off any excess wire.

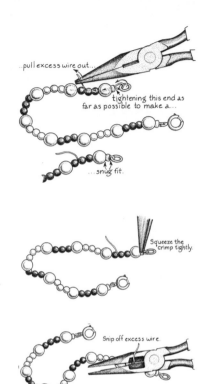

A beaded necklace or bracelet makes a great gift and, of course, is a fabulous way to add to your own trove of jewelry.

ABOUT THE AUTHOR OF
PORTRAITS OF LITTLE WOMEN

SUSAN BETH PFEFFER is the author of both middle-grade and young adult fiction. Her middle-grade novels include *Nobody's Daughter* and its companion, *Justice for Emily.* Her highly praised *The Year Without Michael* is an ALA Best Book for Young Adults, an ALA YALSA Best of the Best, and a *Publishers Weekly* Best Book of the Year. Her novels for young adults include *Twice Taken, Most Precious Blood, About David,* and *Family of Strangers.* Susan Beth Pfeffer lives in the town of Walkill, New York.

A WORD ABOUT
LOUISA MAY ALCOTT

LOUISA MAY ALCOTT was born in 1832 in Germantown, Pennsylvania, and grew up in the Boston-Concord area of Massachusetts. She received her early education from her father, Bronson Alcott, a renowned educator and writer, who eventually left teaching to study philosophy. To supplement the family income, Louisa worked as a teacher, a household servant, and a seamstress, and she wrote stories as well as poems for newspapers and magazines. In 1868 she published the first volume of *Little Women*, a novel about four sisters growing up in a small New England town during the Civil War. The immediate success of *Little Women* made Louisa May Alcott a celebrated writer, and the novel remains one of today's best-loved books. Alcott wrote until her death in 1888.